A WANDER IN THE WOODS

Stories Of Imagination

Edited By Allie Jones

First published in Great Britain in 2021 by:

 Young**Writers**® Est. 1991

Young Writers
Remus House
Coltsfoot Drive
Peterborough
PE2 9BF
Telephone: 01733 890066
Website: www.youngwriters.co.uk

Printed and bound in the UK by BookPrintingUK
Website: www.bookprintinguk.com
YB0465QZ

FOREWORD

Welcome, Reader!

Are you ready to take a Wander in the Woods? Then come right this way - your journey to amazing adventures awaits. It's very simple, all you have to do is turn the page and you'll be transported into a forest brimming with super stories.

Is it magic? Is it a trick? No! It's all down to the skill and imagination of primary school pupils from around the country. We gave them the task of writing a story and to do it in just 100 words! I think you'll agree they've achieved that brilliantly – this book is jam-packed with exciting and thrilling tales, and such variety too, from mystical portals to creepy monsters lurking in the dark!

These young authors have brought their ideas to life using only their words. This is the power of creativity and it gives us life too! Here at Young Writers we want to pass our love of the written word onto the next generation and what better way to do that than to celebrate their writing by publishing it in a book!

It sets their work free from homework books and notepads and puts it where it deserves to be – out in the world and preserved forever! Each awesome author in this book should be super proud of themselves, and now they've got proof of their ideas and their creativity in black and white, to look back on in years to come!

CONTENTS

Cumran Primary School, Clough

Caolan Reid (11)	55
Flynn McAleavy (8)	56
Ryan Stevenson (9)	57
James-Gerard McAuley (10)	58
Cruz Miller (8)	59

Fitrah Southampton Islamic Primary School, Southampton

Maryam Abdulkadir (8)	60

Hauxton Primary School, Cambridge

Khadija Usman (8)	61
Zenab Usman (11)	62

Maldon Primary School, Maldon

Lily Pennick (9)	63
Storm Thurling (9)	64
Samiya Barker (10)	65
Izzy Latchford (7)	66

Mary Exton Primary School, Hitchin

Lucie Rayner (8)	67
Emily Harries (9)	68
Isabella Boyle (8)	69
Matilda Kirupairatnam (11)	70
Zoe Morgan (9)	71
Ava Kemp (10)	72
Bella-Rose Stoughton-Cavallo (8)	73
Hibah Shaheen (10)	74
Isla Skeggs (9)	75
Atharv Bagga (9)	76

Mortimer St Mary's CE Junior School, Mortimer

Beth Matthews (11)	77
George Murphy (8)	78
Lily Price (11)	79
Phoebe Lambert (10)	80
Emily Davidson (8)	81
Annabelle Lambert (10)	82
Jack Murphy (10)	83
Sophie Kempson (9)	84
Noah Verster (10)	85
Annabel Baker-Gabb (10)	86
Alba Cairns (7)	87
Esmie Mackay (8)	88
Lorraine Quarterman (9)	89
Ben Fordham (10)	90
Sarah Furey (10)	91
Alexandra Hoile (9)	92
Luke Brown (9)	93
Olly Bargus (8)	94
Amelie Clemison (9)	95
Ben Carless (11)	96
Holly Randall (7)	97
Violet Hawkins (11)	98
Josi Porter (10)	99
Eva Steele (8)	100
Tia Porter (9)	101
Melissa Everied (9)	102
Isla Hulett (8)	103
Isabella Lloyd (7)	104
Isabella Fordham (8)	105
Aayla Harlow (7)	106
Ruby Hayward (7)	107
Alice Moran (10)	108
Daisy Downer (10)	109
Lucas Hicks	110
Finlay Harlen (7)	111
Sam Martin Thomas (10)	112
Kian Evans (10)	113
Taylor Scutter (9)	114
John Webb (8)	115

Platt CE Primary School, St Mary Platt

Lucas Wyatt (11)	116
Annabel Zeevaart (11)	117

Ravensden CE (VA) Primary School, Ravensden

Nathaniel Howe (10)	118
Paige Davenport (9)	119
Holly Jessica Brydon (9)	120
Chloe Stanton Smith (10)	121
Dylan James (9)	122
Alex Sawyer (10)	123
Leo Bell (9)	124
Oscar Peter Poniatowski (10)	125

Shebbear College, Shebbear

Ashton James Saltmarsh (9)	126
Tyler Douglas (9)	127
Emily Gifford (10)	128
Harry Sibry (8)	129
George Belford (9)	130
Xavier Diffey	131
Max Turner (8)	132

St Paul's CE Primary School, Winchmore Hill

Julia Gosling (8)	133
Tabitha Byrne (9)	134
Francesca Coles (9)	135
William Roberts (10)	136
Felix Buchanan (8)	137
Elodie Gascoigne (8)	138
Elsa Rosa Nussey (10)	139
Molly Harbott (8)	140
Hannah Makombera (10)	141
Elyssia Ions (8)	142
Annellise Brown (10)	143
Alex Boon (9)	144
Samuel Taylor (8)	145
Leo Schramm (10)	146

Olivija Zlatar (8)	147
Emiliana Panteli-Matter (7)	148
Isla Brasnett	149
Xavier Lazarus	150
Naomi Jones (9)	151
James Hunter-Jones (10)	152
Maggie Thompson (9)	153
Evangeline Rees (9)	154
Ben Caton-Jenkins (9)	155
Leo Salah (8)	156
Amy Storey (8)	157
Maya Abe (8)	158
Emily Ellis (7)	159
Hannah Silverman (7)	160
Ethan Dempsey (7)	161
Adam Perera (9)	162
Ed Buckle (7)	163
Isabella Eldridge (8)	164
Tala Chartouni	165

THE
STORIES

The Scary Woods

One day, a little boy entered some magical woods. Suddenly, trees appeared behind him! He was petrified! "What will happen to me? Argh!" Suddenly, monsters attacked him from all sides. He was terrified. "What will I do?"
Then a ninja appeared and took out all the monsters and took the boy back to his house.

Benjie Williams (8)

The Seven Dwarves And Snow White

You know Snow White, right? Perhaps you remember us too? Dwarves with cutsie names!? We're peaceful self-respecting, somewhat reclusive brothers inhabiting these quiet woods. Bernard, Horatio, Simon, Sandoz, Desmond and Darwin. And I'm Garth. Utterly disrespecting our feelings, she dubbed us: Bashful, for Bernie's an introvert; Happy, his facial tics; Sneezy, his pollen-allergy; Sleepy, the star-gazer who compensated for his sleep in the daytime; Doc, his bottle glasses; Darwin's certainly not Dopey! And finally, I took offence to this callousness and remarked the princess should bunk with the three pigs next time. That makes me Grumpy!

Aadhira Singh (8)
ACS Cobham International School, Cobham

The Haunted House

On a dark night, a brother and sister went to a funfair. They decided to go in the haunted house. The sign said: *Come in if you dare.*

"This might be too scary, are you sure?" the girl said worriedly.

"Don't be a scaredy-cat!"

They went in and saw ghosts and ghouls, dolls and clowns. They went up, down, left and right, it was so fast the wind howled. The brother and sister came out of the haunted house, they looked back but the haunted house was gone! On the ground just a doll was left. It winked. They ran!

Caitlin McCulloch (10)

ACS Cobham International School, Cobham

A Small Girl With A Big Dream

Once there was a girl called Jessica. She had a big dream of going on a great adventure.

The next morning, Jessica woke up... and she was still in her bedroom. Then suddenly, a flash of light appeared and *boom!* She went flying through the air and landed on... her bedroom floor. She opened her eyes wider and found a bit of green moss! "Oh cheesesticks!" Her brother had left it there a couple of days ago. Then she walked to her desk, opened the drawer... and there was the most magnificent story of all magnificent stories!

Tessa McVey (9)
ACS Cobham International School, Cobham

Alex And The Alien

I was crying in a field. I'd been bullied by the bully Max and now I was sitting alone. I heard cows in the distance. I picked up a blade of grass and suddenly it started to shake. A round object floated over my head, a green figure came down and greeted me croakily. "Hello Alex, I'm here to make you feel better and to face up to the bully. My name is Alien. Please can you take me to your home?"

"Uhh, I don't know, are you going to kill me?"

"Of course not! I'm the friendliest alien!"

Alessandro Verre (10)

ACS Cobham International School, Cobham

The Lost Girl

One day, there was a kid who could breathe fire and saw some snow. She sighed, "It's too cold!" and her fire made some vapour that was hot! Then she found a fairy toadstool. Allie-May the fairy came out, she was going to see the squirrels. The fire-breathing girl was lost. She looked in all directions, she was sad and embarrassed. She cried, "I am lost!"

Then Allie-May the fairy was pointing to the North Star and said, "Follow the North Star." So she followed it and she was home.

Zahra Zeynalova (7)
ACS Cobham International School, Cobham

Adventures Of Fat Baby

Fat Baby's a dog. Here's one of her adventures. Fat Baby and her friends were playing with a ball. One of the dogs threw the ball into the mysterious shed. Fat Baby went to the shed and discovered there was a monster. At first she got scared and tried to fight it but it didn't work. So she decided to be friendly and asked for their ball. It said okay. It also said it was a he and his name was Jerry - he was lonely and wanted a friend. Fat Baby felt sad for Jerry and became his friend.

Tilly Rymarczyk (8)
ACS Cobham International School, Cobham

The Wild Year

Once I was running from a pack of wild wolves. Suddenly I came to a lake where I saw a leap of different leopards sprinting towards me. I took my only chance and jumped on a thick branch of a tree. The wolves' pack named Catahi could not climb the trees, but leopards can and the leopards followed me up. I could see for miles. I winked at the leopards and together we all swam across the lake until we got to a wild area in Kazakhstan. Here there was thick snow and animals to eat and water to drink.

Alfie Cooling (7)
ACS Cobham International School, Cobham

A Wander In The Woods

Me and my friends are at home, so I ask, "Do you guys want to go for a wander in the woods?"
They said, "Yeah sure."
"We will only be gone for an hour," I said.
It was now five days later and we had only got one bottle of water left! I said, "Come on, this way, I know where we are, we will get out of here in no time." I didn't tell them I actually didn't know where we were and it was all my fault...

Yousef Tawfik (7)
ACS Cobham International School, Cobham

The Mysterious Doorway

On a bright, sunny day, I noticed quicksand in my backyard. It led to a different world and I had to figure my way out after I accidentally fell in. Suddenly, I was in a forest, I saw a path to a door. I ran to it, only to see an endless hallway of doors and a sign that said only one door was correct. Each door was decorated. I saw a sign on the last door so I ran towards it. I opened it and I fell through the door into a cloud... I found gold too!

Ryder Fox (7)
ACS Cobham International School, Cobham

Gone

Me and my mum were going for a walk in the woods. We walked for a few hours, it was starting to get dark. But what we didn't know was we were so deep in the woods that we were lost. We turned around and walked as fast as we could, the moon was up, it was dark. I could hear wolves, I was so scared. I was holding my mum's hand, then through the woods I could see the way out! We walked faster until we got out of the woods!

Aria DeTrask (8)
ACS Cobham International School, Cobham

A Mysterious Hike

One day, Sophia was on a hike with her family. She heard something so she followed it. All of a sudden, the sound was getting louder. She wanted to get closer to it. She ran back, but she felt something was following her. She ran really fast but something got her! She realised that it was a ghost! She couldn't see it. It captured her. She gave the ghost a potion that would turn it good. So the ghost took her home.

Sophia Martin (8)
ACS Cobham International School, Cobham

My Least Favourite Part Of My Life

One dark night I was out. I was at a building, I was there for a party. After the party I went out and fell into something. I saw a lot of light. I was like, "Where is all of that light coming from?" Then I figured out I was in another dimension. I was shocked! I did not like it there. Just then I found a rope, it was leading from the sky. So I decided to climb it. I saw the building again. I was out!

Lucian Menzer (8)
ACS Cobham International School, Cobham

The Knight

A knight was wandering in a spooky place. Suddenly he heard a scream. He ran as fast as a racing car and suddenly he saw a fire! He panicked, then he saw a dragon. He got his bow and arrow and he was going to shoot it in the wings, but then he saw it had a princess so he thought if he shot it the princess would die...

Alexis Taylor
ACS Cobham International School, Cobham

The Big Smash

One day, Hulk was smashing the city and everyone was hurt. Then, a brave kid stood up for people. He went and said to Hulk, "Let's duel!" Then Hulk went near Lark, the boy, and Lark then touched Hulk and he went flying away! After that, the president made Lark a knight. They lived happily ever after!

Felipe Silva (7)
ACS Cobham International School, Cobham

Lost Magic

A girl named Magic and her family went to the forest to go camping.
She got lost and was shouting!
Then she remembered her dad had said if she was lost to stay in the place.
Her dad found her, she was happy.

Mariam Zakaria Abdelkader (7)
ACS Cobham International School, Cobham

Grunga's Revenge

Walking inside the forest, Jason saw nothing except for a hole in the ground. He shuffled closer and got pulled in by a green hand.

All the elves gathered around looking for Grunga had caught.

"Who are you people?" exclaimed Jason. "And why did you take me?"

Grunga used his large arms to pull himself over. "Revenge," grumbled Grunga. Grunga's father had searched the overworld and never returned.

Grunga pulled out a sharp rock, but before it touched Jason a young elf named Auron stopped Grunga. "I hear the short ears above, they're filling the hole. He can stop them..."

Cian Spratt (11)

Bracoden School, Gamrie

Enchanted Forest

I went to the forest for a walk but I saw this glow, so I followed it. I'd never seen this part of the forest before. Just then I had a flashback. I recognised the waterfall and lights, then I heard an elf shouting, "Welcome back to the most popular elf!"

I got very confused.

"Here's the sword," the head elf announced.

"What do you mean?" I asked.

"Wait, you don't know who elf-ra is?"

"Nope," I answered.

"Your family are elves and they were elf-ra. You are the next elf-ra, now take the sword and save our enchanted forest!"

Esmee Twatt (10)

Bracoden School, Gamrie

The Goat

"Have you seen the new leader?" she whispered.

"Who Steve?" he exclaimed.

"Yes, him!" she replied.

As Steve was the new leader he decided to build a lookout.

Two weeks later when all was going well, they saw a bright green light coming towards them. In the lookout they decided to investigate. When they found it they saw a goat drinking green acid, but they didn't know the goat would be their greatest enemy.

One day, they decided to try and kill the goat, the goat struck Steve so they sent tonnes of arrows at him. Thud, the goat died.

Mason Dalgarno (11)

Bracoden School, Gamrie

Wonder Woods

It was a dark day. The sun had disintegrated into gloomy clouds and Logan had his eyes locked on the forest that stood before us. As soon as we walked in we were greeted by three boys.

"You'll need this," said the first boy whose name was Stewart.

"This place is haunted I tell you, as haunted as a shadow!" shouted the second boy.

Logan interrupted, "Poppycock! You're filling our heads with lies!"

And with that the three boys walked back into the darkness of the woods, but in my hands laid an object - a bright ominous crystal...

Ellie Adams (11)

Bracoden School, Gamrie

Bringing Back The Tradition

One lovely autumn afternoon, the sun was shining like a firebolt. Two best friends, Summer and Holly, were having a walk at the edge of the forest. Suddenly, they heard a branch snap. Cautiously, they ventured deeper into the forest and found a magical world full of creatures. Soon after, a creature kindly greeted them, they'd met the boss of the creatures, Fuzzy the huffefluff. She explained that centuries ago their families had joined together and were the rulers of the forest and kept every creature safe. Finally, after a long talk, they decided to restart the tradition.

Aleisha Ritchie (11)

Bracoden School, Gamrie

The Cursed Woodland

As I step into the dark woodland, I notice almost instantly that something isn't right. The fog on the ground is unusually warm and the patches of moonlight piercing through the trees seems unusually bright. While I'm walking deeper into the woods, my cat Kevin is following closely behind. He stops and looks, completely terror-struck, like lamb to the slaughter. Suddenly, a loud shrieking noise comes from a nearby hollow tree, sending a shiver up my spine. Surprisingly, a huge spirit pops out from the tree and gives chase after me and Kevin. Fortunately, we make it out.

Grace Adams (11)
Bracoden School, Gamrie

The Wonderful Woods

There were elves living in the trunk of a tree with a stone that held the tree together. A stone as bright as the sun.

It was a normal day, everybody was happy and everybody was doing their jobs until they realised the stone had been stolen.

"Alfie, the stone is gone!" said the guard.

"My brother!" said Alfie.

The whole tree had collapsed.

"We need that stone!"

Alfie went in the castle, he snuck in and got it back. He ran to their home and returned it to the tree and their home was saved!

Alfie Murray (10)

Bracoden School, Gamrie

The Nutty Nuts

One day, an eleven-year-old squirrel named Charlie was collecting hazelnuts for his group the Nutty Nuts, to make Nutella the chocolate spread. Suddenly, humans came and stole the nuts and chopped down their tree.

"Uh-oh!" Charlie shouted.

He went back to his group and told them. After all of that they went after the nuts. A while later they found them and knocked all of them out and stole back the nuts.

After they got back they gave some nuts to the old wise squirrel and they then set up and made Nutella chocolate spread!

Charlie Murray (11)
Bracoden School, Gamrie

My Home Almost Gone

My parents are fighting. I leave. I decide to go to the only place I call home. It's as comforting as a feather bed, so I go for a wander in the woods. Suddenly, everything has changed. All I can hear is everyone screaming, "Help us!" The forest is burning, I need to do something! I round up all my creature friends by counting one by one. We run out of the woods everyone worries until it is ordinary again. I head home, my parents are happy again. Suddenly, all the weight has lifted off my shoulders. No more tears!

Megan O'Neill (11)

Bracoden School, Gamrie

Wailing Woods

A boy called Mason went into the woods called Wailing Woods, where one blood-bottling goblin called Stew would catch people and bottle their blood. Stew found Mason eating blueberries and invited Mason to a feast, but he was the feast for Stew! But Mason knew he was going to do that... Mason went to the cottage and was shy like a sleepy squirrel, the goblin asked him to go outside to get some soup as he was planning to throw him into the boiling pot and eat him! Mason threw the goblin in the pot and ran far!

Logan Baxter (11)
Bracoden School, Gamrie

The Shifting Portal

Once, on a bright summer's day, I was walking through the trees when suddenly the ground began to shake. I was thrown into the air then down through the soil. I stood up and just about saw the top of a house in the distance. As I walked towards it I heard rustling in my backpack. I opened it and something small, purple and furry hopped out and into the trees! I caught up with it. It was a small purple bunny. Suddenly, a deafening roar split the air. A ninja cat leapt out of the trees! "Fight!"

Samuel Long (10)
Bracoden School, Gamrie

Lost In The Woods

I woke up, clueless where I was. I looked around, there were trees, lots of trees. I suspected I was in a forest. I hoped I wasn't alone so I got up and looked around. As I looked my face became numb. Luckily, I spotted a fire, it seemed like someone was here. I decided to walk further. As I walked raindrops hit my head, I looked around and noticed a cave, I decided to run towards it. When I entered a voice said, "Escape now!" I ran, I was as terrified as a tortoise! Suddenly, I blacked out...

Tegan Underwood (10)
Bracoden School, Gamrie

The Lost Spirit

One night in the wonder woods a fox came out from under a bush and looked around cautiously. It crept out into the bioluminescent light of the mushrooms. Suddenly there was a loud bang! Then all the birds flew away into the night sky. He searched around aimlessly looking for somewhere to hide. He hid in a hole but he was spotted. Next thing he knew, he was in a cage and put on a cart and shipped away. As he left he spotted a small pond, he found a way out and jumped into the pond and disappeared...

Katelynne Thomas (11)

Bracoden School, Gamrie

The Knights Win Again

Shhh! Here come the knights and Steward is leading Mason, Jeff, Tom and Jerry. They are very brave, but the bravest is Dexter. The weakest one is Logan. The leaves are moving and the twigs are snapping and here comes the goblins. They are rushing and charging at the knights and the knights swing, slash, swing, slash. The goblins are defeated and at the end the trees are whistling like a whistle. There is a big cheer, but Jeff is dead. The knights are very sad, the funeral is sad.

Stewart Smith (11)
Bracoden School, Gamrie

The Lovely Woodland

Three young boys are on a walk in a forest. Their names are Jason, Bob and Jess. They're having a nice walk, looking at the leaves, when all of a sudden... they are caught in animal trap! They are hanging from a tree, there is nowhere to go and no way to get out. The boys remember they have a sharp stick, they get it out of their pocket and they get out. They see someone, they run as fast as they can to get out of the woods and they get home as fast as they can!

Dexter Wiseman (11)
Bracoden School, Gamrie

The Boys And The Abandoned Forest

Without listening, two boys walked out of their house and into an ancient, abandoned forest, which they were not allowed to do. Unexpectedly, *crack!* A branch snapped in the distance. The boys questioned each other, "What was that?" They started to get creepy feelings that there was a ghost around them or someone was following them. In panic, they started running towards their house. However, ghostly voices appeared again, the boys were creeped out. "Arrgh!" An ear-piercing scream came from one of the boy's lungs. But the other continued running away. "Arrgh!" came from the other boy...

Colin Dola (10)
Co-Op Academy Nightingale, Harehills

The Haunted House

It was Halloween, in the middle of the woods was a massive house full of Halloween decorations. It was spooky.

Five teenagers, Isaac, Kelly, Lucy, Ben and Isabelle got their costumes on and went to get pieces of candy. There was one final house, the Halloween house. The main door slowly creaked open, *crreeaak!* They went inside... Suddenly there was a werewolf, it was eating flesh. The teens hid in a cabinet. The wolf tried to track their scents, they were worried. They looked around, there was a rocket launcher... *boom!* The wolf dodged and gave a big roar!

Kai Campbell (7)
Co-Op Academy Nightingale, Harehills

An Enchanted Forest

One lovely day, Cesha and her family were looking for a campsite. Cesha said, "Nature's calling."
"Okay," said Mum.
On the way, running up the mountain, she saw a mist. She ran as fast as she could. At the top she went through the mist. "Wow, this is incredible," she said, "but I am hungry." Luckily, an apple tree was nearby, she plucked one of the fruits and looked for interesting things. "It is so beautiful here!" But when she turned around... "B-b-b-bear! I'm gonna die!"
She ran out the mist.

Ta'liyah Spencer Browne (7)
Co-Op Academy Nightingale, Harehills

The Daring Treasure Quest

One stormy night, I'd guzzled some delicious tea, when suddenly I heard some eerie voices! They were saying I could have treasure if I followed them. Moments later, I found a huge building. Trembling with fear, I entered, only to discover that it was stuffed with treasure! Just then, two hideous ogres emerged from under the treasure and grabbed me by the neck! Just as I was about to collapse I thought of an amazing plan. "I've left some gold outside," I sneered.

They sprinted outside only to fall into a deep hole! I was rich and galloped off home!

Adam Fiaz (9)
Co-Op Academy Nightingale, Harehills

The Game Of Rock, Paper, Scissors

One day, Jimmy went for a walk to an enchanted forest. He was so fearless. When Jimmy got in the forest, he shouted, "Oh no, a monster!" It had jumped out of a portal. The monster was large, his eyes were as big as Rubik's cubes, his teeth were like chainsaws.

"I need to fight him and I know how!" Jimmy said, "Let's play rock, paper, scissors. If I win you go back through the portal, but if I lose I'll leave you alone."

The monster agreed.

Luckily, he lost and went through the portal, Jimmy felt like a hero!

Oskar Paulus (10)
Co-Op Academy Nightingale, Harehills

Worst Fear

Once there was a man who came to a very regretful ending. He was walking through a beautiful forest where birds cheeped gracefully. Even though he could hear the tweeting of the birds, the rustling of the leaves and the children playing, there was still a silence in the air. Then he came to a house and it said on the door: 'Come into my garden'. He walked through the door to the wonderful garden. Abruptly, the garden went topsy-turvy, and he saw his worst fear walking towards him. He spun around, hoping to leave. The door wasn't open...

Heran Yosief (11)

Co-Op Academy Nightingale, Harehills

The Missing Sisters!

Two teenagers were in a forest, they both loved nature, but they were not together they were apart. Lilly was walking in the woods and Lucy was hiding in a bush. When they recognised each other they hugged each other so tight they felt strangled. They had a feast of yummy wildlife, it was delicious.

"You are my missing sister, I have been looking for you for so long!" exclaimed Lilly.

They both stayed happily in the woods. They went on camping trips, roasted marshmallows by the warm fire, they loved this life!

Ayla Zaihid (7)
Co-Op Academy Nightingale, Harehills

A Wander In The Woods

I was looking for an endangered species. I was bewildered when suddenly a creature took my arm and lunged towards a black tunnel that looked like a hamster run. I could hear a strange noise so I gazed down to the little monster, who bravely jumped into the tunnel. Making a brave attempt, I squeezed down the hole. Luckily, I went halfway, then I slipped! I held onto the nearest roots when small hands pulled me and to my surprise it was the rare creature I had been looking for! This was my happiest moment.

Zara Anjum (8)

Co-Op Academy Nightingale, Harehills

A Haunted House

A school went on a trip. They arrived at the woods and made a campfire, some stayed in the bus and others explored the woods. They saw a spooky house. Jack broke into the house. Jack wanted to know what was in there. He tried to escape the house but the door shut tight. So Jack explored some more. Jack found a hidden world of ghosts! He was amazed! He was going to be famous! As he walked up the stairs he was certain the eyes in the paintings were following him. Jack found a secret door, he opened it...

Michael Mufaro Gonzo (8)
Co-Op Academy Nightingale, Harehills

The Twisted Bear

Long ago, a twisted bear lived in the misty, dark forest. Its fur was itchy and smelled of old bark, its eyes glowed cyan and illuminated the night, it had more teeth than you could imagine. It had turquoise boils pulsing out its fur. It had a tongue that dribbled with acid, staining the ground.
One day, it dug with its twirling claws into the brown soil and has lurked within there since. So if you ever go walking in the woods, remember, the twisted bear could be under you!

Hubert Dziewulski (11)

Co-Op Academy Nightingale, Harehills

Getting Lost

In the woods there was a little girl called Mily and her parents. Mily went to get marshmallows. She got them, went back and her parents were gone! So she looked around and she saw a house. She was scared so she went in and inside there was a red button, she ran out the house, it was too scary. She found a torch, she turned on the torch and she saw a wolf. Mily took one step and it fell in a cage. She saw her parents and hugged them and then they went home and had hot chocolate.

Sara Aktar (8)
Co-Op Academy Nightingale, Harehills

A Wander In The Woods

One dark, eerie night I entered the enchanted forest. As soon as I entered the gates shut behind me. I heard the bushes moving, then monsters and goblins came towards me and tried to eat me. I ran and ran as fast as I could, then I stopped to catch a breath. I kept on running, then I saw a tree so I climbed all the way to the top. Then I heard another noise. It was seven wild cats, four squirrels and eight hedgehogs. I thought I was going to die. Luckily I didn't die though.

Gabriella Nti (8)

Co-Op Academy Nightingale, Harehills

The Days Of The Legendary Crow

Birds oh birds, the singsongy (and strange) song that I'm singing in Deathland. Now you may ask how I am in the gracious and sophisticated Deathland. Well I'm not the person to give out spoilers, so read on!

It started when I decided to fly over the savannah (what can I say, I'm a bird!) to gain some trust from the elder. Next thing to happen right out of the blue, was a bullet flying into my wing! Falling down onto the ground was painful, but death was worse.

Chiemelie Onwuegbusi (11)
Co-Op Academy Nightingale, Harehills

Lily And The Wolf

Lily and her mum and dad were sitting near a cosy, crackling campfire in the middle of the woods. There was a wolf, a greedy wolf who was spying on them. Lily wanted a marshmallow so she got one. There were so many so she got a lot, but the wolf came towards them and she ran very fast to get away. The wolf ate all the marshmallows. He was hungry so he ate the whole bag! The wolf chased Lily and her parents, she ran very fast but the wolf was faster. He gobbled her up quickly.

Mahrus Butt (8)
Co-Op Academy Nightingale, Harehills

A Wander In The Woods

One night, I went back to my cottage. Suddenly, the door slammed! Then I heard footsteps. I ran to the door and saw my dad. What had happened? There was blood. Then I saw a man armed with knives. I cried and ran inside. I remembered my dad was a policeman, I took his taser and went to the door. The man turned around and I shot him. I called the police, I felt sad. My dad then slowly opened his eyes and I jumped up and down like a kangaroo! I hoped he'd be okay.

Nathan Semuwemba (8)
Co-Op Academy Nightingale, Harehills

A Wander In The Woods

One beautiful day, my family went out to the spooky, scary forest and had a picnic. I was playing hide-and-seek with my sister and brother, but I went too far and got lost. I heard some howling and I ran deeper into the forest, where there was no sun or light. I began to cry. I was too lost. Then I saw my friends, but they looked different... They had a sack and before they could put me in the sack a big orange monster came and saved me and took me home.

Roxanne Proctor (9)

Co-Op Academy Nightingale, Harehills

A Wander In The Woods

One night, I was in the eeriest forest in the world. I was looking for my dog. Suddenly, I saw a frightening house. I went to investigate and I saw my dog in the house. So I rushed in and to my horror I was standing in front of a witch! She would not let me get my dog so I had to think of a plan. I told her there was something in the burning chimney, then I pushed her in. I got my puppy and we ran away into the deep forest to our home.

Justin Paun (8)
Co-Op Academy Nightingale, Harehills

A Wander In The Woods

Once upon a time, there was an old man and his children. They were walking in the forest when suddenly the children saw a tiger. So they shouted for help. Next they saw a snake and they ran very far away. The old man looked for them, he went this way and that way and the old man found them. They did not know how to get home but a tree told them how to get home.

Maria Ecovescu (7)
Co-Op Academy Nightingale, Harehills

A Wander In The Woods

I was all alone, it was a misty, cold, foggy night. I could hear some eerie wolf creatures flying above me. I didn't like it. I zoomed away from the creatures, I could see them following me. The creatures went back to their forest. I got back to my car and drove off. Phew, that was close.
I got home and fell asleep. I was tired!

Zain Ajayi (9)
Co-Op Academy Nightingale, Harehills

Peter And The Lamp

One normal day, Peter was sat on his comfortable sofa. Suddenly, he heard a noise. He bolted outside and saw a golden shiny lamp. There was a letter saying: 'Caution, do not rub!' Peter thought very carefully and came to a decision. He did not hesitate and with no mercy he rubbed the lamp. All of a sudden, a genie appeared. With a clear voice the genie questioned, "What do you demand?" Peter was astonished and overwhelmed. He uttered, "I want superpowers!"
The genie mentioned to keep this a secret or else there would be consequences. This changed Peter's life.

Vansh Dass (11)
Co-Op Academy Woodlands, Leeds

The Wolf

Once upon a time, there was a wolf, his name was Wolfie. His mum warned him not to go to the bears' house because the bears were really scary. Wolfie agreed and then told his mum he was going for a walk in the woods. He saw a little cottage with the door open. Wolfie ate all the porridge in there. He became very tired so decided to go upstairs to bed. Then he saw Little Red Riding Hood who screamed when she saw him and Wolfie ran as fast as he could out the door!

Alishba Akram (8)
Co-Op Academy Woodlands, Leeds

Kobe And The Fairy

Best friends Kobe, Tia and Amber liked to play in the woods. At the woods together one day, they were all playing, but when Kobe was running fast he slipped and fell down a bank. Then from behind a tree came a fairy. The fairy asked Kobe if he was okay.

"I'm okay, but I have lost my friends."

The fairy helped Kobe up the bank and Kobe found his friends again. They went back to playing and the fairy went home for tea.

Skyla-Rae Adams (7)
Co-Op Academy Woodlands, Leeds

A Class And The Ghosts

One day, a class went to the woods, something moved by itself and they thought it was a ghost. Then they found out there was a ghost at the campsite!
They went on an adventure to a cave and there was a cave drawing and during the adventure the class and the ghost made friends. They got to know each other will and got to trust each other. The teachers also got to know the ghost very, very well!

Retaj Said
Co-Op Academy Woodlands, Leeds

Kidnapped!

One day in the Mushroom Kingdom, Mario was walking when Toad said to him, "Princess Peach has been kidnapped by Bowser!"

"Mama mia!" Mario said and went to save her.

Later, Mario saw something in the sky and that something was Bowser's airship. Mario found a cannon and launched himself onto the airship. On the airship he found Bowser Jr in his Koopa clown car.

"The princess is inside the airship but you'll need to get through us," he said.

Bowser jumped on the airship. "Let the battle begin!" he said.

Eventually Mario beat Bowser and Bowser Jr.

Caolan Reid (11)
Cumran Primary School, Clough

The Adventure With Crackle

I found a magic key, what was it for? Did it belong to a door or a gate? In my garden was a secret door. The key belonged to it. When I opened the door there was a fire-breathing dragon. He was a friendly dragon. He became my friend, I was able to ride on his back and have great adventures. He helped light a fire for us to toast marshmallows. They were so delicious. Every evening we would say goodnight and he would take me home. Crackle stayed behind the door and waited for me to visit.

Flynn McAleavy (8)
Cumran Primary School, Clough

Spy Castle

I was walking in the woods, it was frozen and very slippy. The woods were full of dangerous animals. I came across a castle guarded by a vicious-looking tiger. I sneaked around the back of the castle and found an open window. I reached back through the window and tiptoed inside. I took out my drone and sent it deep into the castle to explore. On my drone I saw the castle full of snowy cattle. A winter wonderland!

Ryan Stevenson (9)
Cumran Primary School, Clough

Spy Machine

A spy had a mission from the chief. His task was to stop a scientist that had gone rogue. The crazy scientist wanted to release a great evil that they called the demi gorgon from another world. But the spy came in at the last moment and destroyed the machine that the scientist had created. The spy defeated his robot and then the scientist unmasked the spy. He was a dark, shadowy figure.

James-Gerard McAuley (10)
Cumran Primary School, Clough

The Mysterious Moan

On a dark and stormy night there was a mysterious moan from somewhere in the forest. What was it? No one knew. A man went to investigate the moan, he went looking for it in the forest. The man looked a bit like a superhero, he was strong and he was 3.7 metres tall.
He went missing! No one knows where he is!

Cruz Miller (8)
Cumran Primary School, Clough

Terrible Night In The Woods

Once, in the dark woods, there was an old metal gate. There were two twins running from a nasty witch! Almost instantly the twins were caught, then out of nowhere leapt a spine-chilling horrible troll! But to their surprise the troll was not after them, he was after the witch. Unfortunately, she didn't run because she thought, what can an ugly creature do to a powerful witch like me? Then the troll gobbled her up! Finally, he took Emma and Emelia to a fancy, exquisite mansion as they had become good friends.

Maryam Abdulkadir (8)
Fitrah Southampton Islamic Primary School, Southampton

The Portal!

Alice darted along the cobbled street, she skipped all the way to the orphanage and knocked politely. "Oh, hi Nat-" Instead her best friend Evie came to answer the door.

"Come on, I need to show you something!" she whispered whilst she pulled Alice. They rushed to her room and Evie pointed to something. It was beautiful.

"A portal!" she breathed.

Suddenly, Alice leapt into the glowing green portal. Evie jumped in and they found themselves in an enchanted world.

"Fairies!" exclaimed Alice. "Oh my gosh!"

The girls had discovered an amazing new world. They would always be here forever.

Khadija Usman (8)
Hauxton Primary School, Cambridge

The Leaf Of Destiny!

Claire and Eva skipped down the path that led into the trees. As usual, the girls were walking through the forest admiring the greenery. All of a sudden, Eva stopped. "What was that?"
"What was what?" questioned Claire.
A squirrel scampered down a tree and suddenly spoke. "Hello!" The squirrel went down the path. Curiously, the girls followed through the trees.
"You are destined to save us!" it cried, making them jump. "Find the leaf!"
Eva stared up - a glowing leaf. She showed it to Claire. Jumping up, the girls managed to reach the odd leaf and restore it home.

Zenab Usman (11)
Hauxton Primary School, Cambridge

The Lost Family

Deep down in the woods one foggy night, a deer family were lost. Suddenly, there was a rustle in the trees.

"Who's that?" mumbled Baby Deer.

Slowly, out crept a wolf with glowing green eyes.

"Don't be afraid my dear friends, I'm Happy Wolf. I want to be your friend. What are you doing here?" he asked.

"We're lost!" replied Mummy Deer.

"Don't worry, my dear friends, I'll sniff the way home through this fog."

After a lot of sniffing and walking, eventually the wolf found their home.

"Thank you!" the deer cheered. "We would've been lost without you!"

Lily Pennick (9)

Maldon Primary School, Maldon

The Enchanted Forest

Storm was walking in the enchanted forest and bumped into a girl called Rosie. "Sorry," mumbled Storm.
"My name's Rosie," she replied, smiling.
Storm smiled back.
"Want to be friends?" asked Rosie.
"Sure!" replied Storm.
They started walking further into the enchanted forest.
Rosie started to act weird and Storm became suspicious and watched her out of the corner of her eye. "You okay?" asked Storm.
"I'm fine," she reassured Storm.
Storm later found out Rosie was a demon and tried to help her have a better life and made sure she had many friends.

Storm Thurling (9)
Maldon Primary School, Maldon

My Wander In The Woods

I remember walking through the woods with the iridescent moon shining down on me. Hearing the noise of the sharp knives around every bend I took. I remember reaching a cabin and the smell of rotting flesh bombarded my nose. Creatures of all sizes all with unique looks surrounded me. It became lovely and such a magnificent place to be at that time. Then it happened. I heard a siren singing voice and it lured me in. I followed. My head started spinning and my heart was beating out of my chest. Then everything went black... And I'm here.

Samiya Barker (10)

Maldon Primary School, Maldon

The Enchanted Forest

I went into the forest to pick some berries for my supper. I came across a magical unicorn. She had a pink mane and tail. She had a white body and golden hooves. She was surrounded by a rainbow. I asked the unicorn what her name was, she said Lilly. The unicorn said I could ride her, so I jumped on straight away! We had so much fun running through the enchanted forest. We saw rabbits, foxes, fairies and loads of other unicorns!

Izzy Latchford (7)
Maldon Primary School, Maldon

The Dragon Of The Magic Wood

One cold, misty evening, two girls were sitting in armchairs by the fire talking about the magic woods. Mia said to Lily, "Let's go to the magic woods to look for jewels."

The woods were dense with no sign of the jewels. Until they turned a corner and saw them in their beauty, guarded by a terrifying dragon.

"The dragon's not roaring, it's crying," said Lily.

"Everyone's always trying to steal my jewels," said the dragon. "I'll happily share them I just wish I could wear some."

Mia's jewellery-making father made the dragon a beautiful glittering crown to wear.

Lucie Rayner (8)

Mary Exton Primary School, Hitchin

The Enchanted, Creepy Forest

As Lily was walking through the forest, she heard a strange noise, but didn't know what it was. Lily started seeing confusing blue objects floating above her. She thought she was in a horror film. Suddenly, there was a creepy ghost following her. Lily was very scared. The mysterious forest started to get dark and gloomy. As she ran back to her house, she looked up and heard something. "Who's there?" she asked.

The creepy ghost started to make weird noises...

People realised Lily was missing so they started to look for her. "Where's Lily gone?" they wondered worriedly...

Emily Harries (9)

Mary Exton Primary School, Hitchin

The Weird Creatures In The Woods

One cold evening, Molly and Dolly were sitting on armchairs by a warm fire. Molly asked Dolly if she wanted to go on an adventure, Molly said, "Yes, let's!" So, the girls went walking on a path. Soon they found themselves in the deep, dense, overgrown forest. It started to get dark, and they realised they were lost and felt scared! Then they saw two weird furry green creatures with big eyes in a tree. One spoke to them, "Don't worry we'll guide you back home, follow us." They happily followed and were soon home, chatting by the warm fire.

Isabella Boyle (8)
Mary Exton Primary School, Hitchin

A Hunt In The Forest

The wind whistled and darkness covered the land like a blanket. Cautiously, I sped into the forest, ready to hunt. In the distance, a small pathway covered with snow unexpectedly appeared. As I stepped my numb feet onto it, eerie lights flickered on the pathway. To my horror, bloodstains were scattered all over it. Running further into the forest, sweat coating my body, I saw a decayed hut standing silently. I could hear strange noises emerging from the distance. I grasped the broken doorknob and as I looked inside, a creature's bloodthirsty eyes stared into mine...

Matilda Kirupairatnam (11)
Mary Exton Primary School, Hitchin

Eve And The Peculiar-Looking Grave

It was a dark and gloomy night and a ghostly storm had just begun. A little girl named Eve crept around the entrance of the cemetery as the lightning struck the sign. She slowly stepped near a peculiar-looking grave and brushed the dust off. As she was reading the grave, she leaned on it and fell in! Eve plummeted down until she stopped suddenly and glanced around to see unicorns on clouds flying around. "Woah!" she exclaimed as she gasped in surprise. Rainbows sang softly to her. She was too busy dancing that she didn't realise she was rising!

Zoe Morgan (9)

Mary Exton Primary School, Hitchin

The Woods

Without a care, I stumbled through the bushes, the branches clawing at my face, drawing red droplets. Life was hard, Mum was getting more and more ill, it would be a miracle if she made it another week. All the pain I had experienced, sometimes I thought about making it end. I always came to this dark, miserable woods, it expressed my life; but today I felt something different in the air: danger. The ancient door screeched open, urging me to move forwards. I had nothing to lose, but that's when I saw it - glistening bloodstains covering the ground...

Ava Kemp (10)

Mary Exton Primary School, Hitchin

The Shark With Bad Teeth

I was at the beach and I had my diving suit, then I heard something so I got my suit on and started to swim. Fish were swimming away so I went in the direction they were swimming from. There was a dark cave and I went inside to investigate it. I kept on swimming until I found a shark! He didn't chase me, which I thought was odd. For some reason he was sobbing. "My teeth hurt," he cried. His teeth were yellow.

"I know! I will brush your teeth!" I brushed his teeth.

"Thanks!"

"That's okay."

Bella-Rose Stoughton-Cavallo (8)

Mary Exton Primary School, Hitchin

It's Not Over...

Nothing seemed right. It was a dark evening with misty fog. It was sunset time and the stars were lit up in the sky. A tall archway stood across a bridge. Across the bridge there was a cemetery with gravestones engraved with 'Rest in Peace'. When I passed through the cemetery I could see skeletons moving. I was frozen to death. I could hear my heartbeat quicken and I struggled to breathe. I heard creepy noises. Suddenly, there was loud thunder in the sky. I immediately ran from the cemetery to the main road. I could hear footsteps...

Hibah Shaheen (10)
Mary Exton Primary School, Hitchin

The Lunar Eclipse

Lily lay in bed unable to sleep. It was a dark and quiet night, the air felt old and maybe even... mystic. Lily decided to go downstairs and get some milk. As she poured her milk she noticed a shadow outside in the forest. Without thinking, Lily ran to investigate. As she stepped onto the grass, the moon shone brightly. Beams of moonlight shot through her body, lifting her into the air. Lily felt majestic and powerful. Suddenly, it went dark. Lily awoke in bed, what an odd dream? She looked at the new glittering moon tattoo on her wrist...

Isla Skeggs (9)

Mary Exton Primary School, Hitchin

The Boy And The Trees

One day, a boy was strolling in the woods when he tried to snap a branch off a tree. He fell down and found he was rooted to the ground. The other trees were walking and talking!

One said, "That boy snapped off my prized branch!"

Another shouted, "He did the same to me!"

The chief tree said, "Let us snap off his branch too!"

Suddenly, the boy woke up and realised it was a dream. From then on he never touched a tree and he had certainly learned his lesson, hasn't he?

Atharv Bagga (9)

Mary Exton Primary School, Hitchin

The Ghost In The Woods

Once there lived a girl and boy named Natalie and Leo. They were on a school trip when Leo heard a strange noise. *Whoooooosh!* "What was that?" he asked. Natalie shrugged. Suddenly, they heard it again.

"Come on!"

They went down a path where it was coming from.

"Wait, how do we get back?"

Now the children were very scared. Without warning, a small, multicoloured object floated past them.

"I want to go home!" yelled Leo.

The ghost approached...

"Arggh!" screamed Natalie.

"Don't worry," the ghost reassured. "I'll lead you back home. Follow me!"

"Thank you!" Leo and Natalie cried.

Beth Matthews (11)

Mortimer St Mary's CE Junior School, Mortimer

The Camping Trick...

"I don't want to go camping, it's boring!" George moaned.

"It will be fun!" said Mum while Dad parked the car at the woods.

It was getting dark and looked spooky. His sister Jessica said, "Let's set up the tent!"

Afterwards, Mum and Dad went to collect firewood and George and Jessica stayed at the tent. Suddenly they heard noises and two ghosts appeared from the gloomy shadows. "Run!" screamed Jessica.

"Wait!" said George. "Look at the shoes... They're not ghosts, it's Mum and Dad!" They all laughed.

"This is fun!" said George as they toasted marshmallows on the campfire.

George Murphy (8)
Mortimer St Mary's CE Junior School, Mortimer

A Wander In The Woods

One day, a little girl named Lily and her best friend Hazel went exploring in the dark, creepy forest next to Lily's nan's house. Half an hour after discovering the depths of the woodland, they came across an old mansion. "Hello?" shouted the girls. The rusted old gate opened and the brave young girls silently went inside. Lily and Hazel slowly walked up the creepy drive.

"Knock then!" shouted Lily.

"Shhh, okay," answered Hazel.

Once Hazel had knocked, the old door opened. The two girls went inside, it was dark. The door slammed behind them. What would they do now...?

Lily Price (11)

Mortimer St Mary's CE Junior School, Mortimer

The Secret Door

Richard crept into the woods, the key still enclosed in his hand. Unsuspecting, the rocks ahead formed a wooden door, leaves hugging it. He cautiously approached and with hands trembling, slotted the key into the lock. He turned and thrust the door open and was consumed by a layer of thick dust. Before him glared a pair of piercing blood-red eyes. A rasping voice bellowed out his name, "Richard!" He felt a hand grab and drag him down...

Suddenly, he awoke back in his tent. "Just a dream!" he sighed.

Then the same eerie voice called out again... "Richard!"

Phoebe Lambert (10)
Mortimer St Mary's CE Junior School, Mortimer

The Unicorn's Magical Day

In the magical woods lives a kind unicorn. One day, a ghost comes to the woods. When the unicorn sees it she screams because she is worried it is going to take her horn. If she loses her horn, she won't have any magical powers left. As she turns to run away, she stumbles and hurts her leg. The ghost glides quickly towards the unicorn and helps her up. The unicorn's surprised and thanks the ghost. The unicorn says, "You're not scary, let's be friends!"

The ghost says, "I would love that!"

The unicorn and ghost will remain friends forever.

Emily Davidson (8)

Mortimer St Mary's CE Junior School, Mortimer

The Fire Spirit

Thrilled, I crept into the mystifying forest. I'd longed to explore the vast expanse of acres that were so dense. They concealed the secrets living inside. Branches of ominous trees groaned as the ferocious wind whistled through their leaves. All of a sudden, a secret figure materialised and shielded its hideous face with a torn, hooded cloak. The trees erupted into an explosion of immense flames. Still ablaze, a fallen branch knocked me out and I woke outside my tent. I looked up and saw smoke billowing out of the forest. From then on, I obviously avoided the enchanted woods.

Annabelle Lambert (10)
Mortimer St Mary's CE Junior School, Mortimer

The Woodland War

Kyle hated the developers, they wanted to bulldoze the woods to build houses. Kyle lived in a treehouse in the woods with his animal friends, he couldn't let this happen! He knew the developers thought the woods were haunted, so every night he crept into the construction site to cause mischief. He hid things, moved tools around and took bolts from machinery. The developers didn't know what was happening and were scared. One night, Kyle left a message in red paint looking like blood: 'Leave the woods alone!' The next morning, they packed up and left. Kyle had won!

Jack Murphy (10)

Mortimer St Mary's CE Junior School, Mortimer

A Wander In The Woods

Once upon a time, there was a girl called Red. She lived in a small village in the isolated woods. One morning, a lady came screaming, "Wolf, a huge wolf!" Everyone gathered around pondering what was happening.

The next night, Red woke up surrounded by guts, flesh and blood. She screamed in fear wondering what could do such a thing. Then she noticed the blood dripping from her mouth and the blood of the human heart staining her white dress. She couldn't remember anything but when she removed her blood-red cloak... pitch-black! She was the big bad wolf!

Sophie Kempson (9)
Mortimer St Mary's CE Junior School, Mortimer

The Fox

Briskly, Ardryan stepped outside of his campervan, clutching his coat while in awe at the woodland surrounding him. He eagerly donned his boots and darted toward the foreign landscape. He explored the gloomy forest until he was at the heart of it. Then something caught his eye... a fox. Its hackles raised as it stared wide-eyed at a clearing in the trees. Ardryan's jaw dropped as he saw what stood in front of it... a bear! Adrenaline pumping, Ardryan pulled the yelping fox into his arms and sprinted back to his campervan. He hastily locked the door and drove away.

Noah Verster (10)

Mortimer St Mary's CE Junior School, Mortimer

The Wrong Turn

Two children called Marcus and Stephanie were walking in the woods. They started arguing about which way to go. Out of nowhere, it became dark. Suddenly, a cyclops appeared through the mist. They grasped hands in fear. Its single evil eye glared at them. It shouted, "Destroy!" Marcus came to his senses and picked up a bug-infested branch and he threw it like a spear. It pierced the centre of its eye and the children sprinted away as fast as they possibly could. They found their way back to the sunlight, forgetting their arguments and were good friends again.

Annabel Baker-Gabb (10)
Mortimer St Mary's CE Junior School, Mortimer

A Creepy Camping Trip

One day, there was a dad and a mum and daughter. They all decided to go on a family camping trip. In the evening it was dark and creepy. All was quiet, and then they heard a horrible, horrific noise!

"What was that?" the daughter said.

"I don't know," the mum replied.

The dad turned around. "Argh!"

A monster was standing behind him!

They all ran home as fast as they could.

"Phew!" the dad said.

But what they didn't realise was that the monster was now under the daughter's bed...

Alba Cairns (7)

Mortimer St Mary's CE Junior School, Mortimer

Amy And The Magical Unicorn

One sunny day, a girl called Amy was going camping. She helped her family get their things together. She was so excited and couldn't wait to get there and help set up the tent.

After they'd finished getting their campsite ready, Amy spotted some white dust on the floor. It just so happened to be magical dust, so Amy decided to follow its path. When she reached the end she met a lost, magical, colourful unicorn. She couldn't believe her eyes and asked the unicorn if they could be friends. The unicorn was so happy, they became best friends forever.

Esmie Mackay (8)
Mortimer St Mary's CE Junior School, Mortimer

A Wander In The Woods

Father Bear went to write in his diary after twilight...

'Dear Diary,

Honestly, people's manners these days are disgraceful! I had this pretty girl, looking as if nothing mattered in the world but her, I think her name was Goldilocks - that suits her, barge into my territory and now my poor wife is mortified! Although, what do you expect from humans? She anonymously bullied my son as well! Well, with all this said, at least my outing adventure for berries was spectacular...'

"Yes, coming dear!" yelled Father Bear to his wife.

Lorraine Quarterman (9)

Mortimer St Mary's CE Junior School, Mortimer

The Biggest Bone

A clever dog decided to do magnificent things. He wanted to go back to dinosaur times and get a big bone! Using a watch, kennel and lightning, the dog zapped back to when dinosaurs roamed the earth. Quickly searching for a bone, suddenly he heard a terrifying stomp. *Roar!* It was the mighty T-rex. Shaking like he was in Antarctica, the brave dog spotted a bone and his eyes twinkled. He ran and grabbed it but the T-rex chased him. Frantically, he ran to his kennel, tapped his watch and *poof*, he disappeared just when the T-rex opened his mouth!

Ben Fordham (10)
Mortimer St Mary's CE Junior School, Mortimer

Disappear

I'm Lucy and my friend Emma vanished two days ago. It all started when we were playing in the woods. It began to get dark, so we planned to go in soon. Suddenly, beautiful ghostly lights appeared from nowhere. Emma began playing with them. They enjoyed it, but then they formed a bubble over her. Suddenly, *poof*, she had gone! I'm now running away from the lights, they're after me. I make sure I'm not alone. Today I'm walking with a friend but the lights are already here. I'm Tia and my friend Lucy disappeared two days ago...

Sarah Furey (10)
Mortimer St Mary's CE Junior School, Mortimer

One Weird Night

Olivia's dream came true today, to walk into Cambria Forest. The forest was eerie and she stared suspiciously at the trees. She was mesmerised by the faces in the trees. A hand brushed her shoulder and she became sleepy. She had fainted. A ghost swept past her, Olivia was dying. A light appeared, Olivia was floating above the ground and she realised she too was a ghost. Something pulled her out of the forest, there was her house she'd left minutes ago. Lights were on, they would be worried. How could she tell them she was okay, when she wasn't!

Alexandra Hoile (9)
Mortimer St Mary's CE Junior School, Mortimer

Gotcha!

Luke and William were in the woods late at night with owls tweeting and foxes fighting. The boys were very hungry and went in search of food. Suddenly, a net fell on them, tumbling them into another world where time stopped. The world was full of quests with objects such as tree stumps, stepping stones, a fallen tree bridge and a building of a raft to get over the lake. With one challenge left they searched over rocks to build their raft then looked behind them. Who did they see? The one-eyed and the one-legged pirate of the woods...

Luke Brown (9)
Mortimer St Mary's CE Junior School, Mortimer

The Hidden World

Bang! The caravan door flew open. Tom ran into the woods, his feet pounding the dewy grass. His parents said to never run off again but they were gone, he was free. As he ran, the warm summer breeze blew against his face. He didn't care where he was going, he just wanted to get away. Tom tripped, stood up and looked around. He realised he was no longer in the forest but a magical world. The scenery was beautiful! He smelt burning, turned and saw the forest on fire. Tom needed to stop it but couldn't do it alone...

Olly Bargus (8)
Mortimer St Mary's CE Junior School, Mortimer

Evil To Good

Once upon a time, there was a little wolf. Unfortunately, there was a virus and his friend had to isolate. As Little Wolf was kind he decided to take some goodies to his friend. He set off but on his way, a mean girl called Scary Red Riding Hood said she'd poisoned his friend. Then she vanished! The next day, he heard a knock on his door. It was Scary Red Riding Hood with his friend. "I'm sorry I was horrible, I've left Scary Town to live here so I can be nice like you!" They became life-long friends.

Amelie Clemison (9)

Mortimer St Mary's CE Junior School, Mortimer

A Wander In The Woods

The pale faint sun began to start its descent for the evening, illuminating the dense forest. The sky was full of beautiful pinks and oranges. Far below, a small figure of a girl could be seen walking back towards the entrance of the vast woods. She brushed her hair out of her brown eyes and refused to give up. After 25 minutes of calling Thomas' name and trying to find him, Sam had stopped shouting for her little brother. As she bent down to tie her shoelaces, she noticed a footprint on the ground. She was not alone...

Ben Carless (11)
Mortimer St Mary's CE Junior School, Mortimer

A Wander In The Woods

Fresh from a day at Diddy TV, Rose came home. Rose decided to go for a walk in the woods. When Rose was walking she found a book. "Wow!" she cried. Rose opened the book and all of a sudden a unicorn appeared. The unicorn called Melody showed Rose the one and only Wizard of Oz... Santa Claus. Santa showed Rose the elves but they weren't elves, they were mermaids. The elves showed Rose how to make presents and wrap them, it was like being in a dream! After a while, Rose had to go. She was disappointed to leave.

Holly Randall (7)

Mortimer St Mary's CE Junior School, Mortimer

The Christmas Tree In The Woods

Dear Diary,

I was out walking when... *bam!* I was in the woods. I was very confused. I kept walking and realised there was a big tree in front of me and weird objects all around me. There were baubles and there was a Christmas tree waiting to be decorated. I started decorating it but there was one shiny bauble I couldn't get to. I then accidentally stepped on a toadstool and... *boing!* I bounced up and found myself in bed. Thinking this was all a dream, I looked down and saw a bauble in my hand...

Violet Hawkins (11)
Mortimer St Mary's CE Junior School, Mortimer

A Wander In The Woods

A little dog was chasing a squirrel into the wood. After a little while, the puppy got lost and he sat down and cried. Suddenly, a swirl of golden light appeared. With a pop, a tiny fairy appeared. "Don't be afraid little one, my name is Queen Golden Dust and I am here to help you!" The fairy blew gently on the trees and they magically moved apart. The little dog ran straight out of the woods and into his owner's arms. The little dog was so happy and he licked his owner's face over and over again.

Josi Porter (10)

Mortimer St Mary's CE Junior School, Mortimer

Ava's Amazing Adventure!

"Mum and Dad, can I please go for a walk in the woods?" Ava asked.

"Yes!" answered her dad.

She was walking through the woods when she saw some gates. She opened them and walked in. In the far corner, she saw a nest. She looked closer and saw lots of animals.

After a while of playing, it was time for Ava to go back. When she walked back to the gates, she found out they were locked. Luckily, a kind bird offered to fly her back to the camping site and she said, "Thanks!"

Eva Steele (8)

Mortimer St Mary's CE Junior School, Mortimer

Horror In The Wood

'Twas a normal day that turned into a mystery! In the busy city of Rome lived the beloved Emperor David and his pretty wife Gracie. One day, they both disappeared. It was kept secret but soon some children went to look for them in the dark woods. They followed the trail to a cave. As they got to the entrance, a giant three-headed dog jumped out and gobbled them up whole! As they sat in the beast's stomach they saw the bones of two people with clothes like the emperor and his wife. Soon they understood!

Tia Porter (9)

Mortimer St Mary's CE Junior School, Mortimer

The Mystical Deer!

Once upon a time, there were two kids who were on a camping trip. They were on a lush green field near a creepy wood. They saw a deer and started to follow it into the wood. Glora tried to stop Mitchell her younger brother but she couldn't. They stopped at the feet of a king deer and ran into the woods. Mitchell was captured, Glora saved him by unlocking the cage with a key. They went back to the campsite and did not speak about what had happened that night. Once they had left, they never went back!

Melissa Everied (9)

Mortimer St Mary's CE Junior School, Mortimer

Little Grey Granny Wolf!

Once, I lived as a wolf called Granny Wolf. One day, I was walking in the woods and I saw a girl called Little Red Riding Hood, she was with her friend Mr Wolf. Granny Wolf really wanted to eat Little Red Riding Hood. She took a dive for her. Luckily Mr Wolf ate Granny Wolf up. Yum! Then they both celebrated and had slices of cake. Mr Wolf couldn't eat anything because he had eaten Granny Wolf. Then Mr Wolf spat Granny Wolf out and ate the badness from her. After that, they were friends again!

Isla Hulett (8)

Mortimer St Mary's CE Junior School, Mortimer

Colour Catastrophe

Once, a little girl was walking in the dark gloomy woods when she came across a beautiful bright rainbow. The rainbow was very low to the ground so she wanted to climb it. The little girl was climbing up and came across an enormous rain cloud that she wanted to pass. She used all her strength to blow the cloud away, it worked but she was tired! The rainbow was wet and she slipped and slid down the other side into a castle. When she looked around it was similar to her home. Was this all a dream?

Isabella Lloyd (7)
Mortimer St Mary's CE Junior School, Mortimer

The Very Friendly Ghost

It was a dark night, not a star in the sky and Charlotte was wandering through the woods deep in thought. Suddenly, she heard a noise in the trees. She jumped, it was a ghost! Scared, she started to run but something stopped her. The ghost was crying. Charlotte asked the ghost what was wrong, he said he was friendly but everyone ran from him. Charlotte wanted to fix this so started talking and spending some time with him. They became the best of friends. Sometimes things are not what they seem!

Isabella Fordham (8)
Mortimer St Mary's CE Junior School, Mortimer

Lusia's Walk

Lusia was out walking in a freezing cold field when she saw a copse of ancient trees which were lit up by the sun. She stepped into the circle and all at once she felt as if she'd inhaled the flames of a bonfire. It was hard to breathe. The heat made her feel sleepy but she was worried that if she fell asleep she would never wake up. She had to escape. She tried running but the heat made her slow. Somehow she got back to the field and was welcomed by the cold air and could breathe again.

Aayla Harlow (7)
Mortimer St Mary's CE Junior School, Mortimer

A Pegasus In The Woods!

I was in the woods on a camping trip. I was having a lovely time because I had a flaming fire. Soon it was bedtime and I snuggled up with my mummy and daddy. Suddenly, I heard a noise that was like a horse neighing. I left my tent and stood still like a statue, sharply breathing. Was it a horse? Wait, no, it had wings! Wow, it was a beautiful Pegasus! I said to the Pegasus, "I'm going to name you Sparkle!" Ambitiously, I jumped onto Sparkle's back and she took me away.

Ruby Hayward (7)

Mortimer St Mary's CE Junior School, Mortimer

The Fairy Tree

I was walking in the Irish woods, the stream was gently flowing among the rustle of auburn leaves crunching beneath my feet. As I was walking, I saw a patch of grass and a tree was growing on the patch of sparkly grass. I stayed there for a few minutes. Suddenly, a fairy appeared, it had glowing green wings with intricate swirls and a bunch of curled brunette locks. More fairies started to come into sight as well as a yellow portal. As more fairies came out of the portal, I walked in...

Alice Moran (10)
Mortimer St Mary's CE Junior School, Mortimer

The Sound Of The Howling Wolves!

One bright morning, Jessica and Philip were camping in the woods when they heard a howl. They started to run and run, but got trapped, they had found a dead end! "What should we do now?" asked Jessica.

"I don't know," replied Philip.

All the six wolves transformed into humans. Suddenly the six humans who were the wolves changed back into wolves again. Philip and Jessica ran and ran and the wolves fled. Jessica and Philip never saw the wolves again.

Daisy Downer (10)

Mortimer St Mary's CE Junior School, Mortimer

Lumberjack

Once upon a time, this boy named Jack, aged 12, got angry at his dad for quitting his lumberjacking job. The boy lived in a woodland cottage and because he was angry he ran far into the woodland, vowing never to go back.

A year later, another boy went into the woods and saw Jack with a red and black jacket on and he had an axe on his shoulder. He ran off and the other boy ran back to his cottage where he found his parents lying dead on the floor. He then called the police...

Lucas Hicks
Mortimer St Mary's CE Junior School, Mortimer

The Kind Werewolf

One night, I wandered in the woods under a full moon. Suddenly, a scary werewolf appeared from behind a tree. It didn't attack me, instead it put out its right paw for me to shake. Next morning, I saw a werewolf hunt and was worried about my new friend. I went to warn it but I was hit by a dart. When I woke up, the werewolf had gone. I snuck into the hunt base and stole the key for the cages. The kind werewolf smiled at me and I freed it. I built it a treehouse to live.

Finlay Harlen (7)
Mortimer St Mary's CE Junior School, Mortimer

A Wander In The Woods

Let's make this clear, if you don't know my friend
Al, well, you are going to find out about him in this
story...
He went into the woods one day and he got lost.
He spotted a light in the distance and he followed
it. It led him to a castle where he met a knight who
was pointing an arrow at a Satnav device. Al
picked it up and it led him home. His parents told
him not to do it again.
You can now see that my friend Al is very
adventurous!

Sam Martin Thomas (10)
Mortimer St Mary's CE Junior School, Mortimer

A Wander In The Woods

On a disgustingly hot day in the desert, Alfred, Amelia and Tom all walked down an isolated path until they stopped abruptly. There in front of them was a large colossal hole. They had made a crucial mistake, they had dived into another world. It was amazing! It was full of flying cars and flying people. They were scared but finally they saw a magical portal. As quick as a flash they rushed towards the portal but could they get to the portal in time...?

Kian Evans (10)
Mortimer St Mary's CE Junior School, Mortimer

The Haunted Hut

Sam and his dad went camping in the woods. They arrived at a haunted hut.

Sam woke in the night and could hear the sound of the wind howling. Suddenly, the door blasted open, this woke up his dad. Sam didn't like it any more and asked to go home.

As they were driving away, Sam said, "We are not going there again!" Then he closed his eyes, hoping to have a hot chocolate when he got home.

Taylor Scutter (9)
Mortimer St Mary's CE Junior School, Mortimer

The Creation Facility

Once, a boy was searching a big wood island and then the boy found a golden box. He went into the box and it was a cage with hay. He soon figured out how to work it, he touched a few controls and it made him an otter. Then he made more and more otters and he made them all build a mansion. He then made them live there with him and they were all together and they all lived happily ever after.

John Webb (8)
Mortimer St Mary's CE Junior School, Mortimer

Bad Luck

Years 5 and 6 walked into the dense and gloomy forest. As usual, we each spun at the redwoods tree to transform into our woodland creatures. But tonight it didn't take place! We tried and tried but it didn't work. Questioning ourselves why it wasn't working, we then spun around another tree. The trees stood up with their roots supporting them, branches closed to protect themselves, they then battled taking knocks to the head. Crying out loud, sadly the redwood lost and we walked away with guilt.

Lucas Wyatt (11)
Platt CE Primary School, St Mary Platt

The Willow

One day, Emily and I were on a camping trip. At night, we went into the woods to explore and we noticed a massive willow shimmering. It had a door in the trunk and we went through it. As we came out the other side we saw a new woods that had masses of mythical creatures crowding around a vast injured dragon. An elf standing nearby shouted, "Please help the king!" Emily was a great vet so we agreed to help the dragon.

Soon the king was well and he said as a reward we could come anytime.

Annabel Zeevaart (11)
Platt CE Primary School, St Mary Platt

The Strange Creature

One crisp spring morning, two children called Jack and Sally strolled into a neighbouring wood where they were going to have a scrumptious picnic. They ventured into the cool forest where they settled behind an ancient pine tree. Minutes later, they were eating their sponge sandwiches. Out of a gloomy, coal-black cave came a low growl. Jack tiptoes towards the source. He swept back the vines. "Argh!"
Sally sprinted towards and startled the creature inside the cave. It was a minuscule emerald-green dragon with a petrified face. Then all of a sudden, they were all swept into the abyss...

Nathaniel Howe (10)
Ravensden CE (VA) Primary School, Ravensden

Peter Pan Lives!

I'm walking into the dark, gloomy woods. They're normal. I spring across the calm, snowy branches as my cat self. Yes, I can turn myself into any cat on Earth. Wait a minute, I hear Bigfoot! Yikes! Suddenly, I see a portal and I jump through it. Wow, I'm sitting on Captain Hook's ship! I am sort of worried and I don't know what to do.

"Walk the plank Pan!"

Oof!

I have to save Peter Pan!

I distract the pirates, giving Peter a chance to escape. My plan worked and everybody was safe. Then I returned home.

Paige Davenport (9)

Ravensden CE (VA) Primary School, Ravensden

The Mysterious Madness

Today it was Eve's tenth birthday, so her mum Sarah took her on a surprise camping trip. They packed sandwiches, a tent and some clothes.
When they got to the camping site they were the only ones there. Eve thought about exploring the mysterious wood and her mum said yes, as long as Eve came back that evening.
She started looking at a dead flower patch and then bumped into this mysterious man. His name was Jack and he said, "Do you want to come to my treehouse?"
Guess what? She said, "Yes please!"

Holly Jessica Brydon (9)
Ravensden CE (VA) Primary School, Ravensden

Lost In The Woods

One bright sunny morning, a large primary school went to a forest for a camping trip, but what they didn't know was a five-headed demon haunted the forest. After all the children got off the bus, three best friends called Angelina, Chloe and Summer went to a clear patch of dirt surrounded by trees. They put up their tent and went in for an hour or two for some food. But when the three girls came out of their tent a five-headed demon was staring at them, lifting his hands with nails as sharp as knives.

"Hello..."

Chloe Stanton Smith (10)

Ravensden CE (VA) Primary School, Ravensden

That Thing

Once upon a time, there was a group of six children and they went to play in the woods, but something was off, it was really quiet. Then one of the children disappeared and they thought it was just a prank. So they carried on walking. Then they noticed that three other children had disappeared so they started to panic. As they started to panic, they saw a tall human figure scuttling around the trees. They ran into a cold dark cave and saw their friends tied up. They untied them and ran away really fast.

Dylan James (9)
Ravensden CE (VA) Primary School, Ravensden

What Happened...

Yesterday I went camping. Let me tell you what happened.

Me and my friends were trying to make a campfire. I went looking for some sticks, I must have been gone for hours but I didn't have a watch on me or anything else. I had to go over to a certain spot in the woods to get a certain type of stick for the campfire. Before I knew it, I was lost! In the distance I could hear shouting, like they were looking for someone. I walked towards the commotion, smoke and shouting. Then I saw it...

Alex Sawyer (10)

Ravensden CE (VA) Primary School, Ravensden

The New Dimension

Once upon a time, a kid was having a peaceful walk in the woods. He accidentally opened a portal to a whole new dimension full of aliens of all shapes and sizes. The kid wasn't sure what he should do. Should he jump into the portal? He had to make a decision. He decided to jump in. Had he made the right decision, or had he made a horrific mistake? He landed and the first thing he saw was a one-eyed, eight-armed green alien! Was it friendly? Was it naughty? What was he going to do?

Leo Bell (9)
Ravensden CE (VA) Primary School, Ravensden

Wonder Woods Nightmare

An F1 driver had to do a really hard track, the wonder woods. He went to one-shot qualifying and ended up 5th on the race. In the race he got a really good start but then in the pits on lap 27 he went on the hard tyres but he was fighting for 5th against Alex Albon. He won the position then his team told him to pit again on lap 65 where he switched to the soft tyres, but didn't realise the risk going on soft. The next lap he crashed and broke his back and fractured his leg.

Oscar Peter Poniatowski (10)

Ravensden CE (VA) Primary School, Ravensden

The Creepy Woods

Last summer, we all went on a camping trip in a tent in the deepest darkest forest. As we were settling down in our tent a loud roar occurred. Dark shadows crept over the canvas. We were terrorised by creepy shapes that looked like gruesome creatures crawling around our tent. We were shaking in fear that the sinister presence might capture us. We waited a while and we slowly unzipped the tent. We peeked out and couldn't believe our eyes. An exceedingly tall and slender man stood before us, lightning struck the ground behind him in a blinding flash...

Ashton James Saltmarsh (9)
Shebbear College, Shebbear

The Tree And Me

My name is Tyler, you may have thought I was an ordinary boy, but you would be wrong. I am friends with a tree called Bydo Casith Mollington. This is how our adventure began...

One day, I was quietly walking in the woods, when I saw a tree move it wasn't just its branches moving. Its whole trunk was violently jumping about. When it realised I was there it totally froze. I screamed, which caused the tree to yell! I then whispered, "Please don't be scared."

That is how I became friends with a tree in the dark woods.

Tyler Douglas (9)
Shebbear College, Shebbear

The Shadow

"Keep up!" shouted the teacher. I looked ahead and my friends had disappeared. I panicked and hurried to catch them up, but I must have taken a wrong turn because suddenly the forest changed. Everywhere was gloomy and dark. *Crack!* I jumped with fear as a twig snapped under my feet. It was cold and spooky and a dark sinister shadow approached me. I froze in fear and my eyes were transfixed on the scary shape. I turned to run and wanted to scream but I couldn't. The sinister shape broke the silence...

Emily Gifford (10)
Shebbear College, Shebbear

Arthur And The Great Sword

Arthur hurried through the haunted forest, he needed to retrieve the ancient sword. Suddenly, he found himself in a dark clearing and to make matters worse, he could see faint outlines of ghosts. He drew his sword and threw it at the ghosts and it killed them instantly. He ran to the centre and leapt to grab the sword. His fingers closed around it. He pulled it from its stand, ran out the forest and suddenly had to grab his hand... it was dying. At least he had accomplished something. He then passed away.

Harry Sibry (8)
Shebbear College, Shebbear

The Strange Day

One day in a dark forest, some kids were playing around and doing dares. One told another to go to the other side of the forest and then come back. So he did, the further he went into the forest, the creepier it got. It got darker and more mysterious, then he heard something further ahead so he turned around and there was a man eating cheese! The boy sat down and started eating cheese with him. He ate it all and said thank you and went back to his friends and carried on with the very strange day!

George Belford (9)
Shebbear College, Shebbear

The Claymore

On Friday, I went to a party. My friends took a dare to go into the woods. I went with them. When I arrived, I saw a dark shadow behind me. Suddenly, it disappeared. There was a whisper, "Find the Claymore sword and save your friends." I knew what I had to do. I spotted something shiny in some grass. The grass vanished and I found my feet in a squelchy bog. My eyes were deceived but I bravely carried on. I picked up the Claymore sword and I knew my friends were safe.

Xavier Diffey
Shebbear College, Shebbear

The Gem

One night a man was sprinting in the dark woods when suddenly he tripped. Five minutes later he saw glowing eyes, so he got up and was somewhere no one had been. He was in a different world, he had to face his fears.

He got up and saw the red glowing eyes again, he sprinted away and saw a ruby-red gem glowing in the moonlight. He touched it... It shot him back! As quickly as a cheetah he touched it again and it shot him back again. He quickly put it on the ground!

Max Turner (8)

Shebbear College, Shebbear

The Twisting Trees

Three children and their parents went for a walk. The children ran after galloping deer.

"Where are we?" asked Julia breathelssly.

"I don't know but Mum and Dad will," said James.

They looked to see their parents but instead saw nothing but darkness.

"I think we are in a forest," said Elodie, petrified.

Without warning, all the trees started twisting and scraping. They were getting closer and closer to the children.

"What do we do?" screamed Julia.

They ran backwards into a deer.

"Can we take a ride?" asked Elodie.

And with that they were galloping back to their parents.

Julia Gosling (8)

St Paul's CE Primary School, Winchmore Hill

Fire Figures

Alfie groaned as his family drove towards 'Green Wood campsite'. Alfie loathed nature and outdoor activities with the potential of no Internet. He loved gaming; living without it would be disastrous! Upon arriving, he lifted his phone up and waggled it around, no service!

Soon the inhospitable night drew in. Alfie stared into the campfire, hypnotised by its dancing flames. He was thinking, *this silly fire, I would rather have a radiator!* Suddenly, the mesmerising fire pulled him in unwittingly. Ethereal figures gathered around him, chanting unfamiliar phrases. Alfie froze in terror as a spear was pressed against his neck...

Tabitha Byrne (9)
St Paul's CE Primary School, Winchmore Hill

Pesky Pixes And Friendly Fairies!

Daisy flopped onto her bed. Unbelievably her surroundings shifted, she found herself in a forest of strange creatures.

"She's arrived, thank goodness!" squealed someone. "Daisy we need your help to stop the pixies tricking us!"

"Of course I'll help you," smiled Daisy.

The voice led Daisy into a clearing, where a posse of pixes was throwing grassballs at each other. Very politely, Daisy persuaded them to be as good as gold, promising the fairies would share their mighty magic with them.

Suddenly, Daisy's vision began to blur. She rubbed her eyes and found herself back at home on her bed!

Francesca Coles (9)

St Paul's CE Primary School, Winchmore Hill

Lost In The Woods

"Charlie!" I yelled frantically as I sprinted through the dark, uninviting woods, my heart beating like a bass drum. I ran aimlessly and stumbled, twisting my ankle. I lay there motionless, thinking I would vomit from the pain. Hearing the rustling of leaves, I called out for Charlie. A toothless figure appeared out of the shadows. "What are you doing here?" the stranger questioned.

"I have lost my dog," I whispered.

The stranger put his hands in his mouth and let out a whistle. Within seconds, Charlie was back at my side.

"Be off with you both," the stranger instructed.

William Roberts (10)

St Paul's CE Primary School, Winchmore Hill

The Bow And The Bear

Whoosh! The quivering arrow sped past Fred's ear. *Thud!* Bullseye! Fred's heart sank as he realised his best friend, and sporting rival, had beaten him in the archery final. Leaving the Scout camp, Fred stormed furiously into the misty, wild woods. The deeper he walked, the more menacing it became. Nervously, Fred glanced behind him. There, just metres away, stood a colossal brown bear, towering above him like a vast mountain. Fred froze. *Swoosh!* Down crashed the bear with a mighty bang. Appearing out of the mist, Fred's brave and heroic friend stood, bow by his side.

Felix Buchanan (8)

St Paul's CE Primary School, Winchmore Hill

A Flash Of Lightning

While playing in the woods, Tom and Zach heard a roaring, rumbling sound. Suddenly, they saw a flash of light, the tree in front of them caught fire; flames flew into the air!

"Run!" yelled Zach.

They looked up expecting to see lightning, instead they saw two terrifying dragons hovering in the sky, fighting. As the monsters blew fire, a deadly mist descended. The boys were trapped! Tom then remembered a magical chant, "Go away blow away." To his astonishment the dragons stopped fighting and flew away, the mist following behind. The boys ran from the woods, never to return.

Elodie Gascoigne (8)
St Paul's CE Primary School, Winchmore Hill

The Snake-Agator

Before me, attached to the body of an alligator, volcanic-red eyes and a fleshy veined forked tongue burst from the creature's snake head. My heart was pounding uncontrollably, I was convinced it would burst out of my chest. The monster's solid steely steps reverberated through the deep dense forest and through my bones. Abruptly, the creature halted, locking its eyes on mine. I tried in vain to command my limbs to run, but they didn't. I plunged further into despair. Then the words, "You will die!" hissed from its blood-red mouth. Alone. Defenceless. On the edge of death...

Elsa Rosa Nussey (10)
St Paul's CE Primary School, Winchmore Hill

The Girl And The Bat

Alexa was playing hide-and-seek with her friends Martha and Molly. Alexa went inside a wardrobe, leaving the door ajar. Martha entered, so Alexa moved back, expecting the back of the wardrobe, but found herself in an enchanted forest. She walked through the wood and suddenly a terrifying, enormous, winged pitch-black bat attacked! Alexa fought and managed to get back to the wardrobe. Molly and Martha said, "Where have you been?"

"Let's just say it's been an adventure!" gasped Alexa.

However, she didn't notice the bat sneaking through too...!

Molly Harbott (8)
St Paul's CE Primary School, Winchmore Hill

The Secret Forest

It was a warm summer's day. As Jessica stepped into her garden she found an ancient wooden door. Full of curiosity, Jessica stumbled into a mysterious world. Words can't describe how amazed she was at the forest, the roots protruded from the ground like witch's fingers and she stumbled over. She let out a blood-curdling cry, then stared curiously at the sky. It had turned dark, and her stomach was churning. Perspiration dripped from her brow in terror as she saw the woodcutter turn into a werewolf. Jessica's foot was stuck in the root. Her heart was in her mouth...

Hannah Makombera (10)
St Paul's CE Primary School, Winchmore Hill

The Haunted Forest

There was an enchanted forest with ghosts and ghouls that nobody dared go in. Then one day some friends went in for a camping trip, not knowing it was enchanted. They roasted marshmallows by the fire, suddenly, they heard a spooky shriek, "I'm going to get you unless you get out of my kingdom!"
Frozen in fear to the spot, they started to feel weird. Their bodies were changing, they were turning to stone! Ghosts appeared but luckily ghost catchers also appeared and saved the children. The ghost catchers killed the ghosts so everyone lived happily ever after!

Elyssia Ions (8)
St Paul's CE Primary School, Winchmore Hill

The Epiphany

As I entered the magical enchanted forest the mystical stars floated in the navy midnight sky. Glistening brightly, piercing through the trees, I stared in awe at the misty magic that stood before me. The frosty wind whipped across my face. All of a sudden, everything went dark, not even one star shimmered. *Swkish!* My dress had been touched. Fear strode through me. Something wasn't right. In a blink it was like an epiphany, all the stars had suddenly turned on. Hugging myself, I felt something on my dress. It was a blood print. I shivered with fright. Who? Where?

Annellise Brown (10)
St Paul's CE Primary School, Winchmore Hill

Death On The Broads

One dark, dingy, damp night in October, a family was aboard a small, slow boat. Lost on the Norfolk Broads, blinded by the darkness at only 4:30pm. They realised they'd taken a wrong turn down the canal. With the only light coming from their phones, which were slowly dying, and the glare of the full moon to guide them back to safety. Unknowingly, they entered an estuary and got stuck in the reeds swaying like trees in a violent hurricane. Using three swift motions, they managed to untangle the reeds from the propellor and continued their arduous journey to hell...

Alex Boon (9)
St Paul's CE Primary School, Winchmore Hill

A Wander In The Woods

His heart thumping, he breathlessly sprinted into the dark, gloomy woods. Behind him he could hear footsteps. Closer and closer. A cabin! He brushed aside cobwebs as he swung open the creaking door. He realised in horror that it was abandoned! He slammed the door, darkness crawled around him. The footsteps came closer and closer, he hid under a battered table. He could hear its breath... Suddenly, silence. He was alone in the spooky darkness. Or was he? The hairs on his head stood on end as a vile voice whispered, "Welcome to Hell, have you come to stay?"

Samuel Taylor (8)

St Paul's CE Primary School, Winchmore Hill

The White Phantom

It was a gloomy dark day, Andrew was wandering in the shady forest after an incident with his car which made him search for the nearest petrol station which for some reason led him into the forest. After searching for many hours, he stumbled across an abandoned wooden shed covered with cobwebs. Andrew peered into the window to find a canister of diesel. Without thinking, he pushed past the door and snatched the damp red canister. The door slammed behind his back! Andrew felt a white hand on his shoulder. He turned around...

Andrew was never to be seen again!

Leo Schramm (10)

St Paul's CE Primary School, Winchmore Hill

Lost Lives

Lily and Rose were having a great time at a summer camp until animals and humans were mysteriously disappearing. A soul-sucking creature was causing the problem by grabbing innocent strollers with its tentacle-like arms to capture them underground. A riddle was given to Lily and Rose by a spirit to be solved in order to get rid of the monster and bring back the missing lives. Through solving the riddle the girls were able to find the ingredients for a potion which appeared to be the cure. The girls managed to fulfill the quest and saved the missing lives.

Olivija Zlatar (8)
St Paul's CE Primary School, Winchmore Hill

Pixie And The Goblin

Once upon a time, in a teeny village, there lived a sweet girl called Pixie.

One day, a mean goblin arrived at Pixie's family's house and cast a spell. Pixie arrived home and found her family had been turned into statues. Pixie decided to go into the enchanted forest to find the Queen Fairy Maribel to help her. Pixie found the magic toadstool and slid down the candy slide into the magical Fairy Kingdom. Maribel brewed a potion which Pixie sprinkled all over her family. They came back to life and the goblin disappeared never to be seen again!

Emiliana Panteli-Matter (7)
St Paul's CE Primary School, Winchmore Hill

The Scary Forest

During a game of hide-and-seek, I found myself wandering around the dark, damp, dreary forest, frantically looking for my family's familiar faces and their sweet honey voices. Peering in the darkness, I saw a haunting shadowy figure coming towards me amidst a mist of wispy smoke, which gripped its hands around my throat. I started to panic and paced forwards quickly. Suddenly, my foot was trapped under a heavy log. The pain seared through my foot. I just couldn't get free. "No!" I screamed as the figure drew closer. I was doomed...

Isla Brasnett

St Paul's CE Primary School, Winchmore Hill

The Ghost Hunt

Once I came across a forest. It was dreary and echoey. As I stumbled into the dark trees, I heard a blood-curdling scream! Quivering with fear, I backed into the shadows like a rabbit in the headlights. Then I saw it. The ghost. It was a horrifying spectre, a dreadful sight. Suddenly, it came after me, chasing me in the moonlight. Then I remembered I had read a book about ghosts. They disappeared if they touched water. I had an idea. I bolted through the woods until I reached a lake. I jumped... The ghost followed.
"Phew!" For now...

Xavier Lazarus
St Paul's CE Primary School, Winchmore Hill

Ghostly Hallows

On a dark and stormy night, three adventurous children were going to the woods. When they got there they saw tall, towering trees and ravens as black as the midnight sky. Then the children stopped in front of a sign that said in bold: *Beware Of Strange Happenings*. The children ignored the sign and carried on with their journey. Suddenly, a bright beaming light appeared then the children saw ghosts. Just as they were about to run as fast as their little legs could carry them, the ghosts threw them into a deep pit and left them there to rot.

Naomi Jones (9)
St Paul's CE Primary School, Winchmore Hill

The Secret Society Of Hunters

Many moons ago, on the streets of London, lived an imaginative boy. He would create things that had never existed until something strange happened... The boy scurried down the streets of London and saw an unusual round object. Little did he know it was no ordinary round object, it was a Zero Point! Cautiously, he touched the Zero Point and ended up in a different world! Dark gloomy fog bit into his skin as he raced past something that made him quite fulfilled. It was a Zapatron 2000! This had belonged to the hunters of their own secret hideout...

James Hunter-Jones (10)
St Paul's CE Primary School, Winchmore Hill

An Autumn Walk In The Woods

Taking deep breaths of the crisp autumn air, I decided to venture to the park. My feet crunching on the carpet of golden-brown leaves, I entered the woods that were on fire with red and golden trees. The wind suddenly picked up, leaves as beautiful as summer flowers took their one chance to soar high into the sky. The wind dropped and they fluttered like butterflies to the ground. A light shower turned to driving rain. I sheltered in the cafe and watched the trees dancing in the wind. I wondered if there was anything more beautiful than autumn.

Maggie Thompson (9)

St Paul's CE Primary School, Winchmore Hill

The Forest With The Evil Curse

Joe and his friends were camping in the woods to celebrate the last year of college. Joe decided that he would go and collect some sticks for the fire. Meanwhile, Joe's friends were sitting in their tent. Whilst Joe was getting sticks, he accidentally stood on a green pressure plate and a potion fell on his head! He wandered around and got more sticks, until he realised that he'd turned into a wolf! Joe started to head back, tracking his steps until he found his friends. His friends cried in shock and helped Joe reverse the evil curse.

Evangeline Rees (9)

St Paul's CE Primary School, Winchmore Hill

A Wander In The Woods

The mist was like an icy breath as the man called for his lost dog. The forest was dark and impossible to get through, until an eerie, greenish light filled the clearing. A terrifying troll looked furious as the dog tried to wrestle something shimmering from his pointy fingers. The man sneakily looped the lead around the troll's feet. As the dog won the battle for the treasure and took off in a victorious sprint with the man, the troll tried to follow in pursuit but his feet wouldn't move and he crashed heavily to the ground.

Ben Caton-Jenkins (9)
St Paul's CE Primary School, Winchmore Hill

A Wander In The Woods

One cold night, I woke up in my bed. I saw a big forest with a shiny gate through the window. I crept downstairs and opened the front door. I walked on the crunchy leaves, it was so dark and scary. When I got to the gate, I opened it and saw a campfire. Suddenly, the fire transformed into a ghost who made lightning come from the sky. He roared, "Rise children, rise!" Hundreds of skeletons rose from the ground, screaming. They started attacking me, but then I was back in my bed. "It was a dream," I whispered.

Leo Salah (8)
St Paul's CE Primary School, Winchmore Hill

The Ghost Train

Isobel came across a pair of big silver gates and was hypnotised by what was behind them. She spotted a gap in the gates and squeezed through. Isobel looked around, all she could see was long, creepy, greenish palm trees. Suddenly, she saw a man shouting, "Buy a ticket!" Isabel bought a ticket and boarded the train. She noticed the other passengers were ghosts! The train started to move and Isobel jerked forward and fell on a ghost. He got very angry and pushed her off the train. She fell on the floor and grazed her knee.

Amy Storey (8)
St Paul's CE Primary School, Winchmore Hill

The Everlasting Haunted House

One cold, dark night I was walking in the forest when I suddenly saw a haunted house! I looked curiously at it, then I glanced around. There was no one in sight, so I tiptoed up to the door and pushed it open cautiously. It made a slight creaking sound. I crept through the door and saw something that looked like an everlasting hallway with infinite rooms. I walked into the first room and it was empty, I checked around 79 rooms and they were all empty! I turned to leave but as I went to open the door... *boom!*

Maya Abe (8)
St Paul's CE Primary School, Winchmore Hill

Going Into The Haunted Forest

There was a girl and a boy who had a sleigh with two unicorns pulling it. They weren't allowed to go too far, but they did. They went into the haunted forest where they met a baddy who had snakes and spiders. They were frightened and they really wanted to go home. Luckily the unicorns were charged up ready to go and they knew the way home.

That night, they went to bed to get a good night's sleep but they had the baddy in their heads so they couldn't. They knew never to go far again!

Emily Ellis (7)

St Paul's CE Primary School, Winchmore Hill

The Magical World

Once there was a girl named Martha and a boy named Dan. They were walking in the woods when they saw a tree, but it wasn't ordinary. It had a swirly thing in it. When they looked closer they were sucked in and they found themselves in a palace. They got out quite quickly and saw lots of animals, and then they saw a dragon. It was dark, a colour they had never seen, and had bubbles with people inside. A little gnome told them they were soul bubbles and soon they found their way back and told their parents.

Hannah Silverman (7)
St Paul's CE Primary School, Winchmore Hill

The Panda Woods

It appeared I was in a bamboo woods. I must have teleported here last night. I found an old campfire and collected some new wood to start it up and keep me warm. The mountains in China could be freezing cold at night. I had to move quick! There was a half-eaten bamboo stick on the floor, who had eaten it? There was a crunching noise in the distance, it started to get closer and closer till an angry panda appeared in front of me. The panda chased me around the whole woods! I had never run so fast!

Ethan Dempsey (7)
St Paul's CE Primary School, Winchmore Hill

The Bewitched Tree

I saved a life today. I was just having fun at the woods and I stopped at a tree to rest because I'd been running for ages. I chose this tree because there was an old cottage to look at. Suddenly, I heard a strange noise coming from the tree, I saw that the branches were moving without any wind. It started to move towards the cottage, which was bad news because I was hiding there. I leapt up high and bit a branch and the tree became normal. The girl in the cottage gave me a chicken bone.

Adam Perera (9)
St Paul's CE Primary School, Winchmore Hill

The World Of Chaos

Jake was in a hidden world when he heard a rustle and looked around and saw nothing. Everything was quiet. Then he saw a terrifying dragon with lots of spikes on it. The dragon started to chase Jake, he ran on and on, ghosts started to chase him too! Then, while he was running, he tripped over a stone from a castle, he stepped in a trap. One leg got caught in a net and a ghost got him. Suddenly, he turned as white as a ghost, then he started to fly! He realised he had turned into a ghost!

Ed Buckle (7)
St Paul's CE Primary School, Winchmore Hill

The Enchanted Forest

A princess was walking in the deep, dark woods and heard a croak. She followed the noise and saw a fog of mist and she couldn't get in but the croak could so she pushed and pushed and she finally saw the croak was a talking frog! She was so scared but managed to keep it in. The frog explained to her how he could talk. Since he was a poisonous frog he was dying, he asked the princess to kiss him but she couldn't because he was poisonous so he died and she felt sad.

Isabella Eldridge (8)
St Paul's CE Primary School, Winchmore Hill

Into The Woods

I was in bed gazing at the woods, wondering what behind all those trees. I got the courage to sneak out into the gloomy woods. I was a step away from the woods, but I heard footsteps behind me. I ran deep into the woods. I was lost and frightened. Then I saw a strange grey house. I knocked on the door. A witch came out. She dragged me inside and told me I had to win a game or I'd be gone. I grabbed my water bottle, poured it over her and she was gone. I ran to safety.

Tala Chartouni

St Paul's CE Primary School, Winchmore Hill

![YoungWriters Est. 1991]

YOUNG WRITERS INFORMATION

We hope you have enjoyed reading this book – and that you will continue to in the coming years.

If you're a young writer who enjoys reading and creative writing, or the parent of an enthusiastic poet or story writer, do visit our website **www.youngwriters.co.uk**. Here you will find free competitions, workshops and games, as well as recommended reads, a poetry glossary and our blog. There's lots to keep budding writers motivated to write!

If you would like to order further copies of this book, or any of our other titles, then please give us a call or order via your online account.

Young Writers
Remus House
Coltsfoot Drive
Peterborough
PE2 9BF
(01733) 890066
info@youngwriters.co.uk

Join in the conversation!
Tips, news, giveaways and much more!

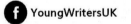 YoungWritersUK    @YoungWritersCW   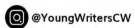 @YoungWritersCW